THE INJURED PUPPY

CINDY PRINCE

ILLUSTRATED BY
ALI PRINCE

BUTTON PRESS

Chapter 1

"Found you!" Sophia said, jumping around the hay bale.

"Not fair—you were peeking!" Justin said.

"I wasn't, I promise."

Justin crossed his arms over his chest, disgruntled. "I'm bored of hide-and-seek."

They'd been playing hide-and-seek for over an hour, so Sophia didn't blame him for being sick of it. Dad had a short morning at the clinic, so he'd dropped the kids off up the road at Granny and Grandpa's farm to play for a few hours. Playing at the farm was one of Sophia's favorite things to do, and now that Justin was old enough to join her without adult supervision, they had complete freedom to explore.

"Do you think we could go play with the puppies?" Justin asked.

"Granny said we could play with them after lunch," Sophia said. "They're being adopted soon."

Justin's face pulled into a scowl. "Which ones? I hope not my favorite."

Justin had tried unsuccessfully to convince their parents to adopt the runt—the tiniest puppy in the litter.

Dad said the kids didn't have time to train a puppy with school starting soon. Mom said she already had a baby to take care of, and she certainly wasn't going to be in charge of another one all by herself.

Sophia leaned back against the hay, still damp and cool from the morning dew. "Do you want to play tag?"

"No," Justin said slowly, flashing a mischievous smile. "I want to climb up there." He pointed above them to the small window of blue sky peeking through the stack of bales.

Sophia put her hands on her hips. "Justin, you're only six. I barely started climbing the bales last year when I was seven."

"I'm not scared," Justin insisted, searching for the perfect spot to start climbing. Sophia hesitated, looking down at her jelly shoes. She really should've chosen better footwear.

Realizing Justin was already halfway up the first bale, she reached for the orange twine that bound the hay together. Wedging her feet into the cracks, she felt the hay poke into her skin but pushed herself upward anyway. It wasn't long before she found an easy path to clamber up to the top. Sophia was about to announce her win when she saw Justin already sitting there next to her.

"Beat you," he said smugly.

"It's only 'cause you're taller," Sophia muttered.

She scanned the farmyard below them. From this vantage point, it felt like she was queen of the world. The chickens were pecking happily in their coop, the ostriches were squawking at each other in their pen, and Licorice, the farm dog, was sniffing curiously around the barn.

"Sophia!" Justin said suddenly, "Are you okay?" She followed his gaze and saw a long scratch on her leg, just above her ankle. "It's bleeding. We should get you a bandaid."

Sophia ran her finger along the scratch and winced. It stung a little but didn't seem to be bleeding *that* much. It wasn't worth climbing all the way down and running up to Granny's house.

"It's fine," she said bravely, looking up. She needed a

distraction so she wouldn't think about it. "Hey Justin, watch this." She turned and assessed the width between the stack of hay bales they'd just climbed and the row next to it. The gap looked smaller than last year, but maybe that was just because she'd grown. Her heart started to pound as she backed up a few steps to give herself a running start. Driving her knees forward, she sprinted and leaped across to the other side.

"Easy peasy," she said, dusting herself off and turning back toward Justin. "Now it's your turn."

Justin's eyes widened. "I don't think that's a good idea."

"If I can do it, you definitely can. You've got longer legs."

"Sophia..." he said, trailing off. Without finishing his thought, he cocked his head to the side and walked toward the edge of the bale. "Did you hear that?"

"What?"

"It sounds like someone's crying."

Sophia's brow furrowed. She hadn't heard anything. She walked toward the edge of the hay and listened with all her might.

"There it is!" Justin said. "It's coming from over there." He pointed past the gate, the trampoline, and the raspberry patch.

She squinted, scanning the green summer grass for anything that could be making the noise Justin described. "I think I see something moving..." she started, and just then, she heard it. A weak whimper floated through the still morning air. "Justin! Look! By the shed next to the house. There's an animal down there. And I think it's in trouble!"

Chapter 2

Sophia climbed down the haystack as fast as she could with Justin close behind. When they reached the ground, they bolted across the hay-strewn farmyard and onto the path leading back to Granny and Grandpa's house.

"Remember, we don't know what kind of animal that is," Sophia cautioned as she ran. "We should never touch an animal we don't know."

"Right," Justin nodded. As they approached the shed, they slowed to a walk.

"Do you see it?" Sophia asked. Justin shook his head. They walked carefully across the grass, now dry and warm from the morning sun, until they spotted something rustling in the dirt next to Granny's favorite Rose of Sharon bush.

Justin gasped. "Sophia, I think that's one of the puppies!"

Sophia peered closer. The creature did look rather small, and she could see white and brown spots, two eyes, and a shiny black nose. "But why would it be separated from the litter?" she asked.

"I don't know," Justin said. "But that's one of my favorites. I can tell by the color of her ears."

Sophia stepped closer, and sure enough. This puppy was the one she and Justin played with all the time. She sighed. "What are you doing outside, little guy?"

She knelt down next to the pup and gently stroked the top of his head. His eyes were drooping, and his tiny body was quivering from tip to tail. Sophia went to scoop the puppy off of the ground, but it yelped as soon as she moved it. She quickly set it back down.

"Sophia, you hurt him!"

"I didn't mean to! I was just picking him up." She felt awful that she may have caused the little puppy any pain. He sat whimpering in the dirt, and Sophia just knew something wasn't right. "Let's get him back with his mom and brothers and sisters," she said. "Maybe he's sad sitting out here all alone."

"But he cried when you tried to lift him," Justin said. "How will we move him back into the shed?"

That was a good question. The puppy seemed comfortable enough lying down. "What if we put something underneath him? Then we could lift him together without making him cry."

Justin nodded, looking around the yard. "What about that?" He pointed to a ripped cardboard box sitting next to the stairs of the deck.

"Hmmm," Sophia said. "I think that might be a bit too wobbly." The cardboard looked old and soggy. Probably not strong enough to hold a puppy. "But that could work!" she said excitedly, jumping up and running toward a small stack of old boards next to the shed.

Careful not to get a splinter, she lifted the top boards to look for a smaller size. She found the perfect one a few panels down and carefully slid it out of the pile. This would work perfectly. Tucking it under her arm, she walked quickly back to the puppy.

"Here you go," Sophia said gently, lowering herself to the ground. She held out the thin board, sliding it along the ground and underneath the puppy's front paws. The puppy looked down, curious. She pushed the board a bit further, and the puppy whimpered.

"I don't think he wants to get on," Justin said, and Sophia nodded.

"He's probably scared. Here, you lift this side, and I'll lift the other. We can move him without making him change positions." Sophia showed her brother how to wrap his hands around the puppy's lower half. "1—2—3," she said, and they lifted together, quickly shifting the pup onto the board.

"I'll lift this side," Justin offered, picking up the back end. Sophia smiled, picking up the front. Together, they stood up, bringing the puppy with them.

"It's a good thing we're about the same height," Sophia smiled triumphantly. Justin grinned as they carefully carried the puppy to the door of the shed.

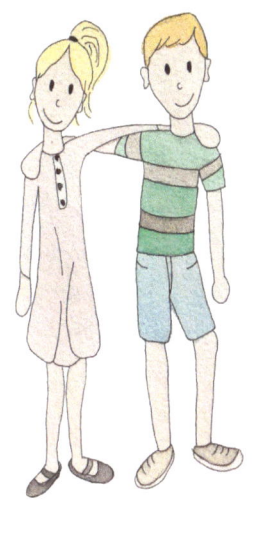

- -

Chapter 3

Holding tightly to the board, Sophia reached behind her and opened the door, then cautiously stepped inside. They could hear the other puppies happily playing and yipping as soon as they walked inside. The sun streamed through the windows, bathing the quaint garden shed with golden morning light.

Justin kicked the door closed so the puppies—now swarming their feet—wouldn't escape. Sophia laughed at their exuberance. "Okay, okay! Just a second, and we'll play with you." Carefully, the children set the board with the puppy down next to his mother. He whimpered and slowly wiggled his way to her side, searching for food.

"Why isn't he acting like the other puppies?" Justin asked, sitting down on the wooden floorboards as the four pups surrounded him. He giggled as they licked and nipped at his fingers.

"I don't know," Sophia said, her brow furrowing. She got down on all fours and inspected the puppy. Before she could get a good once-over, something caught her eye. "Look, Justin!" she said, pointing to the back corner of the shed. "There's a hole in the boards back there."

Justin scooted over to sit next to her, and the puppies followed. Sophia patted the head of a little brown and white spotted pup nuzzling her leg. "Do you think that's how he got out?" Justin asked.

Sophia nodded. "It looks like it's a bit of a drop to the ground. And it's a small hole—maybe the puppy got stuck and hurt himself on the way out." She looked over at the snuggly little puppy, finished nursing, sitting forlornly next to his mother.

Sophia scanned his little body, looking for anything that could give them a clue. As she looked over the side closest to her, she noticed the puppy's front leg was tucked underneath it. "I think he might be injured," Sophia said softly, reaching out to touch the leg. The puppy whimpered as soon as she made contact. "It's his leg."

"What should we do?" Justin asked. Sophia sat back on her knees, thinking. What if his leg was broken? She didn't want to make it worse by touching it. But she also knew it would take a long time to get Dad or Grandpa back to the house. If they could just get the puppy to the Clinic, maybe one of them could help.

Suddenly, an idea occurred to her. "Justin! Remember that wheelbarrow down by the fence?" Justin thought for a second and then nodded. "You stay here with the puppy, and I'll go get it. Then we can wheel him down to the Clinic and have Dad check him out."

Justin grinned. "Great idea, Soph!" Sophia stood up and carefully stepped over the puppies, snuck out the door to the shed, and darted back toward the gate.

She found the red wheelbarrow right where she remembered—propped up against the fence so it wouldn't fill with rainwater. Standing on her tip-toes, she grabbed the handles and carefully lowered it to the ground. It took her a minute to figure out how to maneuver it up the paving stones, but within a minute or two, she was able to keep it steady.

Sophia set the wheelbarrow down at the top of the

path, close to the entrance to the garden shed. She jogged back to the door and went inside.

"Justin," she said excitedly, "Let's go!" Picking up the board they'd used earlier, they worked together to put the puppy on their makeshift stretcher, then carefully carried him outside to their emergency transport wheelbarrow.

"Can I push?" Justin asked, running toward the handles as soon as the puppy was settled.

"How about you push once we get to the road?" Sophia said. "It's going to be hard to push it over the grass."

"But I'm taller and—"

Sophia laughed. "I know, but I've had more experience." She'd pushed the wheelbarrow for at least two minutes already, which made her the expert in this situation. Justin sighed but nodded his head in agreement.

"The road is the most fun part anyway," she said, patting his shoulder and reaching down to grip the handles.

Chapter 4

Sophia pushed the wheelbarrow across the grass, over the gravel next to the house, and Justin helped her lift the wheel over the railroad ties next to the driveway. From then on, it was smooth sailing. The puppy didn't make a sound, even when they hit a bump or tipped the wheelbarrow a bit too much. It was like he knew they were trying to help him.

Sophia gave the wheelbarrow to Justin to push when they reached the road, and she walked next to him, keeping a hand on the metal, just in case he lost control. The street down to the Clinic was downhill, which made it easy to push. Sophia loved riding her bike down this road, but only when Dad had his truck ready to drive her back up the hill to Granny's.

She looked over at the pasture on their left. The herd of sheep was happily grazing in the summer grass. The baby lambs followed their mothers slowly and peacefully in one big family group across the field. Red-winged blackbirds sang merrily as they flitted across the road, landing in the cattails along the ditch.

"I'm getting tired of holding this," Justin said, pulling Sophia's attention from the animals. They were already halfway to the Clinic.

"You pushed a long time!" she said, impressed. "I'll take it from here."

"Sophia!" Justin said, shaking out his tired arms. "We need to give this puppy a name!"

Sophia nodded in agreement. She'd been so worried; she hadn't even thought about it. "Hmmm..." she said, thinking.

"What about Tiny?" Justin suggested.

Sophia giggled. "He's not going to be tiny for long. I'm trying to think of something that shows he's adventurous. Because he tried going outside by himself."

Justin scratched his chin. Suddenly his eyes lit up.

"How about Henry? Like Henry Hudson? He was an explorer."

"That's perfect!" Sophia gasped. "How did you know about that, Justin?"

"From a book we got at the library," he beamed proudly.

Sophia grinned. "I love it. Little Henry, our puppy explorer."

Justin and Sophia walked the rest of the way down the road and carefully turned onto the Clinic driveway. Henry had fallen asleep at some point along the journey, and Sophia smiled at his cute little ears draped along the board.

"I'll go get Dad!" Justin said excitedly, bolting toward the front door. Sophia stopped at the Clinic entrance, set the wheelbarrow down, and waited. The puppy lifted its head and looked around, then let out a whimper.

"It's okay, little guy," Sophia said, petting his head gently. "We're getting you help."

Just then, the Clinic door opened, and Justin walked out, pulling Dad along with him. "See?" Justin said. "We think Henry's hurt. He needs help!"

THE INJURED PUPPY

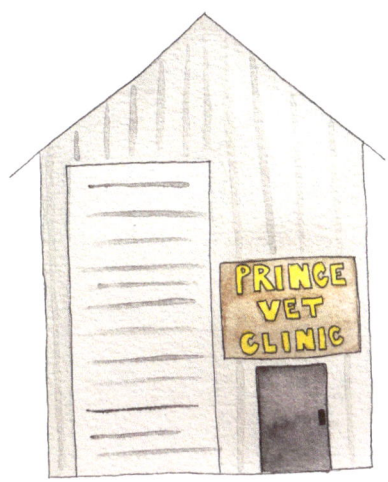

Dad put his hands on his hips and looked up toward Granny's house. "You two pushed this puppy all the way here in a wheelbarrow?" Sophia and Justin nodded. "That's got to be almost a kilometer." He shook his head in wonder. "You must really care about this puppy."

"Henry," Justin corrected.

"Right," Dad said with a grin.

"We think his front leg is hurt," Sophia started in a rush. "There's a hole in the shed, and he was outside all by himself crying. When we picked him up—"

"Slow down, Sophia," Dad chuckled. "I can barely hear what you're saying."

Sophia took a breath and started where she'd left off. "When we picked him up, he yelped. I looked at his paw, and there's a big scratch."

"Alright," Dad said seriously. "Let's get him into an

exam room and take a look." He reached in to pick up the puppy, but Justin stopped him.

"He doesn't like being picked up, so we put him on the board to keep his leg still," Sophia said. "Justin and I can carry him in."

Dad stepped back and opened the Clinic door. "After you," he said, allowing the kids to carry Henry into the waiting room.

Chapter 5

Dad helped Sophia and Justin lift Henry onto the exam table.

"Don't hurt him," Sophia said as Dad reached for the paw Henry was hiding underneath him.

"The truth is, it might hurt him a little bit as I feel his leg," Dad said, pulling Henry's front leg out gently. Henry whimpered. "But we have to make sure we know what's wrong so we can treat it correctly."

Justin's eyes filled with tears. "Does he know we're trying to help him?"

Dad nodded. "Animals might not understand our words, but I think they can tell when people are trying to help them. You two treated him so kindly this morning. He knows we're safe."

Justin nodded, wiping a tear from his cheek. Henry whined as Dad pressed his thumb and forefinger against his bone.

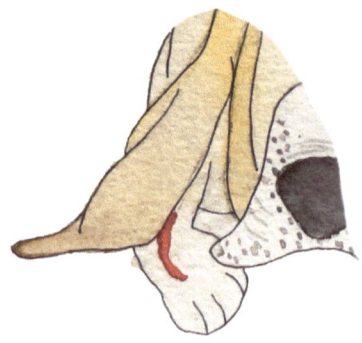

"Right there," Sophia said, pointing. She could see a scratch.

"It's just like yours, Sophia," Justin said. "From this morning!"

Sophia looked down at her leg. She'd been so worried about the puppy she'd completely forgotten about it.

"Yep, you're right," Dad said. "Henry's telling me this spot is tender, but it doesn't feel like it's broken. I think he just got a bad scratch. You said he went through a hole in the shed?" Sophia nodded. "Well, Henry's lucky you two found him. He wouldn't have been safe in the yard all alone for long."

"What do you mean?" Justin asked.

Dad sighed, reaching for a bottle of ointment and a bandage. "He could've gotten too cold, too weak from not having any food, or worse, found by a predator."

"There are animals that eat puppies?" Sophia asked, her eyes wide.

THE INJURED PUPPY

Dad nodded. "Owls, hawks, coyotes, you name it." Sophia shivered. No wonder Granny was keeping the puppies safe in the shed. She said someone had to be with the puppies at all times if they were out in the playpen, but Sophia didn't realize it was because of predators.

"Do you two want to help?" Dad asked, pulling out a bottle of clear liquid and a few pieces of gauze. The kids nodded excitedly, and Dad handed them blue gloves just like his. "Sophia, why don't you squirt the saline solution over the scratch, and I'll clean it up."

Sophia nodded, pulling the gloves on and taking the bottle. She carefully tipped it over. "Will this hurt him?" she asked.

"It might sting a little, just like when we clean up your scratches, but it will feel so much better afterward," Dad said.

"Why do we have to clean it?" Justin asked as Sophia squeezed, allowing the water to drip onto Henry's leg.

"That's a great question," Dad said. "The world is full of bacteria, and when we get a cut, sometimes that bacteria can get inside our bodies and cause problems."

"Like when I cut my toe!" Justin said. "It hurt and got all red."

Dad nodded. "Exactly. Okay, Sophia, I think that looks good." Sophia tipped the bottle upright and handed it back to Dad.

"Your turn," Dad said, looking at Justin as he pulled out a pair of electric clippers.

"Are you giving Henry a haircut?" Sophia giggled.

"Kind of," Dad said. "We need to trim his hair around the scratch so it won't get caught in the wound as the skin heals." Justin reached out and put his hand on the clippers as Dad glided it gently along Henry's leg.

"Perfect, all done," Dad said, turning off the clippers.

"That's it?" Sophia asked in surprise, patting Henry's head. "You did so well, Henry!" she cooed.

"There's one slight problem, though," Dad said, and Sophia's heart dropped. Was there something else wrong with Henry?

Dad sighed. "You may want to think about a different name for Henry."

Sophia and Justin looked up at him in confusion. "Why?" Justin asked. "We named him after a famous explorer."

Dad chuckled. "Be that as it may, our little puppy here…is a girl."

Justin's jaw dropped, and Sophia looked at him in complete shock. "How do you know?" she asked.

"Here," Dad said, motioning for them to come closer. "Take a look." He lifted the puppy's tail and showed the children what to look for.

Justin's shoulders drooped. "Now what are we going to call him? I mean, her?"

"Henry could still be a girl name," Dad said, chuckling. "I just wanted to make sure you had all the information."

An idea occurred to Sophia, and she turned to Justin in excitement. "Justin! I know what we can do! We can call her Henrietta!"

Justin grinned from ear to ear. "So she's still named after Henry Hudson?"

Sophia nodded enthusiastically.

"Well, now that we have that settled, there's one last thing," Dad said. "She'll need to wear this until she heals." He pulled out a thin piece of clear plastic and folded it around Henrietta's neck, making a circle.

Sophia's eyes widened. "What is *that*?"

Dad chuckled. "It's a cone. Henrietta needs to wear it because puppies really like to lick and chew."

"I know," Justin laughed. "They chew on everything!"

"Right," Dad said. "She'd chew on her cut and prevent it from healing. This way, her mouth won't be able to reach her paw."

"But can she see? And eat?" Sophia asked, still very concerned about Henrietta's new accessory.

Justin moved his head from side to side, looking through the plastic. "She can still see, Sophia. Look!" Henrietta's tongue lolled out as she watched Justin, moving her head right along with him. Sophia laughed. It looked like she was already feeling a bit better.

"How long will it take to heal?" Sophia asked.

Dad took off his gloves and reached for his cleaning supplies. "About ten days."

Sophia frowned. "But Granny said the puppies were going to be adopted soon."

"Well," Dad sighed, "I guess Henrietta will have to stick around a little longer than her brothers and sisters."

Justin's eyes lit up. "You mean, she'll need someone to take care of her? Can we take her back to our house?"

"You'll have to talk to Mom about that," Dad said. He reached out and rubbed Henrietta's back. "You've had an exciting morning."

"We all have," Sophia smiled, and Dad nodded.

"Should we get this little gal back to her mom and siblings?" Dad asked.

Sophia and Justin looked at each other with wide eyes. Were they going to have to push Henrietta *all* the way back up the hill to Granny's house? *By themselves?*

Dad laughed out loud. "Don't worry. I have to go check on a horse in town, so I can give you a ride back up the road. We can put the wheelbarrow in the back."

Sophia sighed with relief. "I call holding Henry—I mean, Henrietta—in the truck!" she said, raising her arm high in the air.

Justin scowled. "Sophia, that's not fair! You got to push her most of the way—"

"Hey, now," Dad said. "How about she sits on *both* your laps."

Justin grinned. "I call her head!" He raced out of the exam room toward the front door before Sophia could protest.

Chapter 6

Henrietta was so tuckered out, she fell fast asleep on the drive back to Granny's and didn't even wake up when the kids took her out of the truck.

Dad let Sophia carry her into the backyard, and when they got there, they found Granny outside with all the pups in the playpen. Justin took off running as soon as he saw the fun, but Sophia took Henrietta inside the shed to be with her mom. She didn't think she'd like being jumped on by brothers and sisters at a time like this.

When Sophia walked back out into the yard, Justin was being chased by three puppies at the same time. She laughed, jogging over to join them.

"Looks like you two had a busy morning," Granny said, waving as Dad walked by, pushing the wheelbarrow back to its spot on the fence.

"Granny, Henrietta got out of the shed this morning!" Justin said, collapsing on the grass in a fit of giggles as the puppies climbed all over him, licking his face.

"Now, how could that've happened?" Granny asked, putting a hand on her hip. She looked lovely this morning, wearing light blue pants, a brightly colored shirt with flowers on it, and a wide-brimmed gardening hat over her short, grey curls.

"There's a hole in the back," Sophia said. "C'mon, I'll show you!" Granny stepped over the edges of the pen and followed. "Right there," Sophia said, pointing to the small break in the siding.

"Ah, looks like I'll have to have Grandpa fix that. For now, let's put these here to keep any more puppies from getting curious." She picked up two bricks from the side of the shed and stacked them over the hole. "That's more like it."

Sophia breathed a sigh of relief, knowing that the puppies would be safe. "When are the puppies going to their new homes?" she asked.

"A few will be leaving with their families tomorrow, and the rest will go on Monday afternoon," Granny said.

Sophia pondered this a moment. "What about Henrietta? Dad said it would take ten days for her to heal."

"Well," Granny said, pausing. "I don't think it would be a good idea to send her off before she's ready."

Sophia beamed at her. "Are you going to miss them?"

"The puppies? They're a joy, Sophia, but they're also a lot of work. Which reminds me, I'd appreciate you and Justin helping me clean out the shed and putting down fresh newspaper." Granny winked, and Sophia laughed.

"We'll help," she said.

"That's my girl."

Sophia ran back toward the playpen but stopped short. "Granny, do you think Henrietta could play outside for a bit? Even with her scratch?"

"I wouldn't bother her if she's sleeping, but if she's up, I don't see why not."

Sophia gave a thumbs up and ran to the door of the shed, opening it slowly and peeking inside. Henrietta, still sitting next to her mother, looked up with her wide, chocolatey eyes.

"Do you want to come play outside?" Sophia whispered. Henrietta used her good paw to scratch at the cone around her head. Sophia took that as a resounding 'yes.'

Chapter 7

"Henrietta!" Justin called. "This way! Look, I'm running over here!" He waited for the puppy to drop the stick she'd been carrying in her mouth and pay attention to the new game of chase. When she finally looked up, Justin took off down the grass, and Henrietta immediately bolted after him.

"You might be faster than me, but you're not faster than her!" Sophia laughed, watching Henrietta catch up quickly and jump at Justin's heels. Justin collapsed on the grass in a fit of giggles as the puppy jumped on him, her tongue lolling out.

It had been two weeks since they'd helped Henrietta with her hurt leg, and she'd been able to take the cone off a few days ago. With Mom and Dad, the kids decided to let Henrietta stay with her mother while she healed, but they came every day to look after her and help Granny keep up with the puppy chores. It was a lot less messy in the shed now that there was only one puppy left.

"Sophia!" Justin called, pointing over the sheep pasture toward the plume of dust rising from the road at the bottom of the hill. "Someone's coming!"

"Do you think it's them?" Sophia asked, a pit growing in her stomach. She'd known this day was coming. She knew that once Henrietta was better, she'd be going to live with her new family, but Sophia didn't know if she was ready to say goodbye quite yet.

She ran across the grass to Henrietta and rubbed her ears. "I wish we could keep you," she whispered, covering her soft puppy head in kisses. Sophia and Justin were quiet a moment, petting the puppy they'd grown to love so much over the past two weeks.

"Let's play, Sophia," Justin said. "Let's use all the minutes we have left."

Sophia smiled, wiping a tear from her cheek. "I like that idea." She stood up and took off across the yard, looking for Henrietta's stick. "C'mon, girl! Want to play fetch?" Henrietta panted and loped toward her, a wide, happy puppy smile on her face.

Sophia, Justin, and Henrietta played in the bright morning sun until Granny called to them from the porch.

"Sophia! Justin! Time to bring Henrietta to the house, please!"

Obediently, Sophia scooped up the wiggly puppy and walked toward the back steps.

"Can I carry her, Sophia?" Justin asked. Sophia looked at her little brother, his eyes wide and pleading, almost as big as Henrietta's.

"Sure, Justin. You can carry her once we get past the shed."

When they made it inside, Granny took Henrietta and led the children toward the front door where a family was waiting in the driveway. Sophia peered through the window as they walked but couldn't see the people clearly until they stepped outside.

Her eyes lit up. "Layla!" Sophia said excitedly, running to her friend from school and hugging her.

"Hi, Sophia," Layla's mom said. "What are you doing here?"

Justin crossed his arms over his chest. "This *is* our Granny's house, you know."

Layla's mom laughed. "Of course, how silly of me. Oh!" she said, noticing the puppy in Granny's arms. "Layla, who do you think this is?"

Layla looked away from Sophia and her face lit up. "Is this her? Our new puppy? We've been waiting forever to meet you!" She ran to Granny and stroked Henrietta's back. "Is she all better?" she asked.

"Yep!" Sophia said, walking over to join them. "This is where her paw was injured, but look—it's all healed now." She pointed expertly at the spot where Henrietta's hair still hadn't quite grown back all the way. "We were the ones who took her to the clinic when she got hurt."

"Really?" Layla said in awe. "That must've been scary."

Sophia looked at Justin, and they shared a smile. "Not really," she said. "We're used to this sort of thing."

"Thank you for taking care of her for us," Layla's mom said. She turned and picked up a pet carrier from the driveway and brought it closer. "I think it's time for us to get going home, though. Everyone's dying to meet this little girl."

Sophia looked inside the carrier and saw a soft blanket and a chew toy. She nodded her approval. Layla helped Granny put Henrietta inside the carrier.

"Do you think we could come visit her?" Sophia asked.

Layla grinned. "Yes! You could come over—Justin, too—and we could all play in the backyard! Dad just put up a new tire swing."

"Just have your parents give me a call," Layla's mom said. "We'd love to have you."

She picked up the carrier and put it on the floor in the backseat of their minivan. Layla hopped in and waved before closing the door. Sophia and Justin jumped and waved back until the van had pulled out of the driveway and was well down the road.

"That wasn't too bad, was it?" Granny asked.

Sophia shook her head. "We're going to get to see

Henrietta all the time! I'm so glad she went to a family we know."

"Life has a way of working out that way," Granny winked. "Now how about we have lunch?"

"I want peanut butter and honey!" Justin called, running toward the door.

"We had that last time," Sophia groaned. "How about grilled cheese?"

"Grilled cheese is for winter!" Justin's voice floated out from the entryway.

Granny pulled Sophia's hand into hers. "If you can make it yourself, you can have whatever kind of sandwich you want."

Sophia grinned up at her, gave her hand a squeeze, and ran into the house.

THE END

MORE IN THE PET VET SERIES

The Abandoned Kitten

The Lost Birds

ABOUT THE AUTHOR

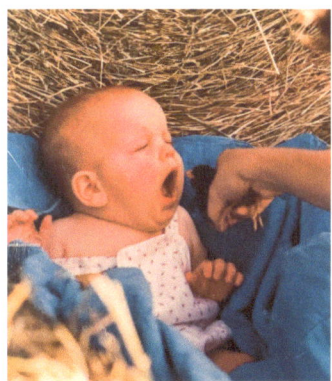

Cindy spent her early childhood in southern Alberta, Canada where her dad and grandpa were the only veterinarians in town. The Pet Vet stories are based on fond memories of her days taking care of pets over the weekend and joining her dad on veterinary house calls.

Cindy currently resides with her husband and four children in the Denver Metro area and continues to foster pets through the Longmont Humane Society. She tries to not keep all of them.

CPSIA information can be obtained
at www.ICGtesting.com
Printed in the USA
LVHW071447050822
725284LV00001B/3